Welcome to the Forest, where
THE MINISTRY OF MONSTERS
helps humans and monsters live side
by side in peace and harmony...

CONNOR O'GOYLE
ives here too, with his gargoyle mum,
human dad and his dog, Trixie.
But Connor's no ordinary boy...

When monsters get out of control,
Connor's the one for the job.
He's half-monster, he's the Ministry's
NUMBER ONE AGENT,
and he's licensed to do things
no one else can do. He's...

MONSTER BOY!

For Anne Ingleby-Lewis

First published in 2009 by Orchard Books
First paperback publication in 2010

ORCHARD BOOKS
338 Euston Road, London NW1 3BH
Orchard Books Australia
Level 17/207 Kent St, Sydney, NSW 2000

ISBN 978 1 40830 244 6 (hardback)
ISBN 978 1 40830 252 1 (paperback)

Text and illustrations © Shoo Rayner 2009

1 3 5 7 9 10 8 6 4 2 (hardback)
1 3 5 7 9 10 8 6 4 2 (paperback)

Printed in Great Britain

Orchard Books is a division of Hachette Children's Books,
an Hachette UK company.

www.hachette.co.uk

MONSTER BOY

GORGON GAZE

SHOO RAYNER

ORCHARD BOOKS

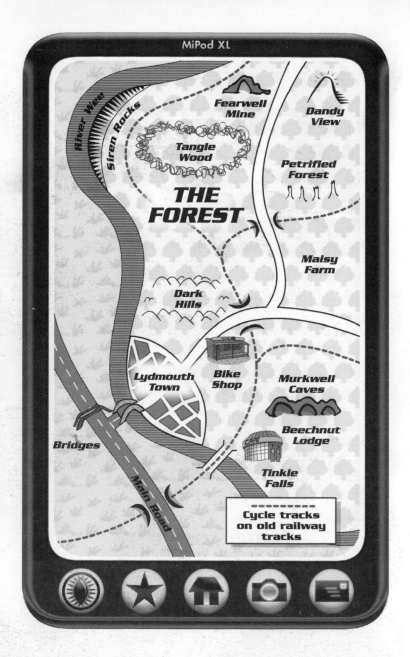

"What is *that*?" said Connor, pointing at a tangled heap of metal.

"It's art!" said his mum.

"Art! It looks like a load of bike mirrors that have been welded together," Connor joked.

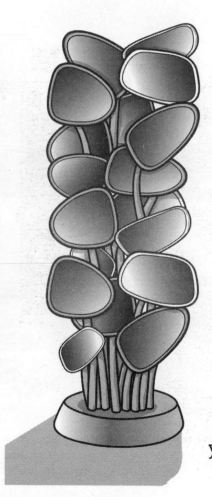

"It might look like that to you," Mum sighed. "It's sculpture. I call it *Don't Look Back*. I'm entering it in the annual Forest Art Competition. I was inspired by your latest Monster Bike upgrade."

Mum looked after Connor's amazing Monster Bikes at the Pedal-O bike shop where they lived. She wheeled MB6, Connor's all-terrain bike, out of the secret bike store.

"Look," she said, pointing at a tiny camera on the back of the saddle. "This will let you see what's going on behind you. You can view it on the handlebar video screen."

"Wow! That's brilliant, Mum."

Just then, Connor's MiPod beeped.

MISSION ALERT!

To:	Monster Boy, Number One Agent
From:	Mission Control, Ministry of Monsters
Subject:	There are reports of trees being turned into stone

We need to stop this now before we end up with a petrified Forest!

Please investigate immediately.

Good luck!

M.O.M.

THIS MESSAGE WILL SELF-ERASE IN FIFTEEN SECONDS

"Got to go, Mum," said Connor.
"It'll give me a chance to test the
rear-view camera."

"Meet me later at the
art competition,"
Mum said. "I'll have
your sandwiches ready.
And do be careful!"
"Oh, *Mum!*"

Connor's mum was a Gargoyle, so Connor was half-monster. His code name was Monster Boy. If anyone could look after himself, Connor could.

"Hold on, Trixie!" Connor yelled. "This bit is really steep!"

"Wuff!" Trixie barked out a warning. The two trees at the bottom of the hill were very close together. Trixie loved riding in MB6's front basket, but she didn't like crashing!

MONSTER BIKE INFO

MB6

You can't always trust what you see in a mirror, so MB6 is fitted with a 20-megapixel rear-view camera.

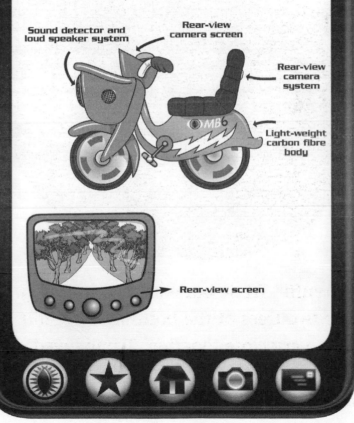

Sound detector and loud speaker system

Rear-view camera screen

Rear-view camera system

Light-weight carbon fibre body

Rear-view screen

"Woooah!" Connor brushed one of the trees with his foot as he expertly squeezed through the tiny gap.

Whu-u-u-mp! Something hit the ground behind him. Connor skidded to a halt. A branch from a tree had fallen to the floor and shattered into tiny pieces.

Connor pressed the slow-motion instant-replay button. He couldn't believe what he saw on the video screen. The branch had missed him by millimetres.

Connor broke a leaf off the tree. "It's made of stone!" he marvelled. I've never seen anything like it."

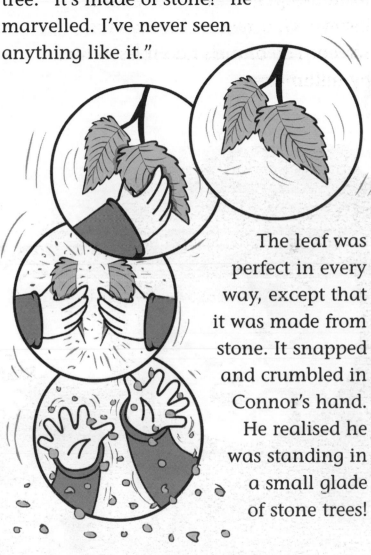

The leaf was perfect in every way, except that it was made from stone. It snapped and crumbled in Connor's hand. He realised he was standing in a small glade of stone trees!

"Wuff!" Trixie had found
something else. She wagged
her tail furiously, calling
Connor over to have a look.

"What is it, girl?"

The ground was littered with what looked like strips of tissue paper. Connor picked one up and examined it.

"Snakeskins?" Connor was surprised. "There are at least thirty of them. I know snakes shed their skins when they grow bigger, but I thought they did it alone."

Connor tapped the screen of his MiPod. "If I type 'stone' and 'snakes' into the Monster Identifier Program, I wonder if it can tell me anything?"

MiPOD MONSTER IDENTIFIER PROGRAM

Monster:	
Gorgon	

Distinguishing Features:
Gorgons look like women but have snakes for hair. They often wear sunglasses.

Preferred Habitat:
Pre-historic Earth.

Essential Information:
Anyone who looks into a Gorgon's eyes will be instantly turned to stone. In Ancient Greece, Perseus defeated a Gorgon named Medusa. He looked at her in a mirror so she couldn't turn him into stone.

Danger Rating: 5

Connor couldn't think where to begin looking for the Gorgon. There didn't seem to be any more clues, so he went to find his mum – and his sandwiches!

"Did you win the art competition?" he asked his mum when he arrived at the gallery.

"Not this time," Mum smiled. "That's the winning entry over there. It's such a delicate piece of work. I don't know how the artist made it."

Connor took a bite of his sandwich and looked across the gallery. A small but perfect stone tree stood on a plinth. Connor read the description.

THE TREE OF LIFE
STONE CARVING
BY GORGON ZOLA

The artist,
Gorgon Zola,
was surrounded
by her admirers.
She was dressed
in black and
wore sunglasses.

Trixie growled at
Gorgon Zola's hat.
A snake wriggled out
from under the brim
and hissed back.
Then everything
happened very
quickly...

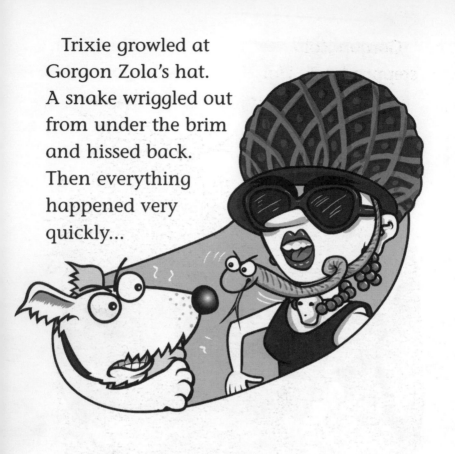

Trixie barked,
spread her wings
wide and flew at
the snake.

Gorgon Zola stepped back. Her hat fell off and her sunglasses tumbled to the floor.

The Gorgon's head was covered in wriggling, hissing snakes! She stared wide-eyed at Trixie.

Trixie froze in midair.
Instantly, her body turned stiff
and grey. Her little wings
stopped beating. She dropped
to the floor like...a stone!

A million thoughts rushed through Connor's mind. Tossing his sandwich away, he dived to catch Trixie before she hit the floor and shattered into a million pieces.

"Everybody, turn away!" he shouted, rolling in front of Mum's sculpture. "Don't look into the Gorgon's eyes!"

Incredibly, Connor's MiPod beeped at that very moment. It was a message from his dad, Gary O'Goyle, the world famous Mountain Bike Champion. He always sent messages at the most unhelpful times!

Hi son,

In Canada for the Rocky Mountain Bike Race. Had an accident in training today. Silly driver backed out of a car park. He didn't use his mirrors!

A few cuts and bruises, but I'll be OK.

Lots of love,
Dad

"Poor Dad," said Connor. "But that gives me an idea!" He put Trixie down carefully and angled Mum's sculpture.

He could see the Gorgon in all the mirrors. Her eyes were shut tight as she scrabbled around for her sunglasses.

"I'm so sorry!" she wailed. "It was an accident. I didn't want to hurt anyone. I just wanted to use my power to create works of art!"

"Look into these mirrors," Connor ordered.

The Gorgon opened her eyes and looked at Connor in the mirrors. They protected him from her gaze.

"Now use the
mirrors to look
behind you,"
Connor said.

Gorgon Zola peered into the bizarre collection of mirrors. Each one showed a reflection of her prize-winning tree.

Slowly, the tree began to change. The leaves turned green. The branches swayed gently as they came back to life.

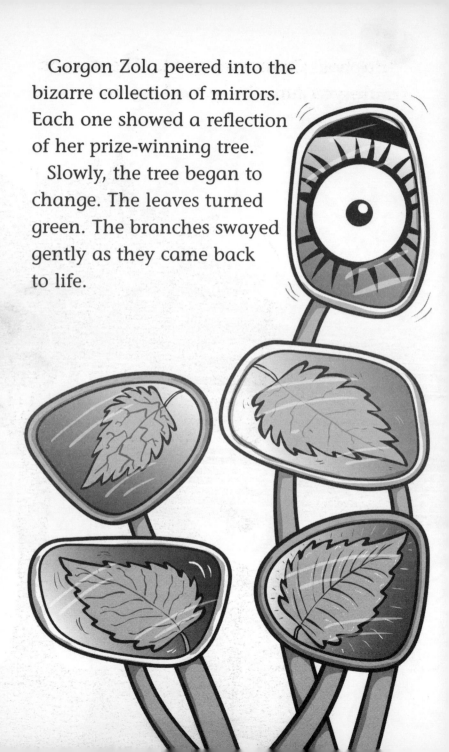

"Ha, ha!" Connor laughed. "The mirrors make you turn things back again!"

Connor angled the mirrors so
that the Gorgon could look at
Trixie. Soon she too had turned
back into a living, breathing dog.

Trixie was thrilled to be alive again. She licked Connor's face and wagged her tail until Connor thought it might drop off!

"I'm so sorry," Gorgon Zola said for the hundredth time. "I'm quite friendly really. So are my snakes...they're only grass snakes, you know."

"Your tree looks even more beautiful now," said Mum. "It still deserves the first prize."

"Only thanks to your sculpture," said the Gorgon. "You are the true winner!"

Later, in the forest of stone trees, Gorgon Zola used Mum's sculpture to turn the petrified trees back to life.

Connor and Mum couldn't watch
directly in case they were accidentally
turned into stone. But with Connor's
rear-view camera on MB6, they saw
everything that went on behind them.

"You two should work together," Connor suggested, once Gorgon Zola had put her sunglasses back on. "Mum can make the sculptures and you can turn them into stone!"

"On reflection," said Gorgon Zola, "that sounds like a great idea!"

"Hisssss!" her snakes agreed.

"Art," said Mum mysteriously, "is like a mirror of real life."

"Wuff!" Trixie barked. She didn't know much about art, but she knew she preferred to be alive.

"Well, stone me!" Connor exclaimed. "Everyone's happy. It looks like the perfect monster solution."

SHOO RAYNER
MONSTER
BOY

All priced at £3.99

The Monster Boy stories are available from all good bookshops,
or can be ordered direct from the publisher:
Orchard Books, PO BOX 29, Douglas IM99 1BQ
Credit card orders please telephone 01624 836000
or fax 01624 837033 or visit our website: www.orchardbooks.co.uk
or e-mail: bookshop@enterprise.net for details.

To order please quote title, author and ISBN
and your full name and address.
Cheques and postal orders should be made payable to 'Bookpost plc.'
Postage and packing is FREE within the UK
(overseas customers should add £2.00 per book).

Prices and availability are subject to change.